D1577565

The Book
of
WIREMU

STELLA MORICE

Drawings by
NANCY PARKER

BLACKWOOD & JANET PAUL
Auckland : New Zealand

ANGUS & ROBERTSON
London

Whaia ko tetahi take pai

Me whai ko te rangimarie

PURSUE SOMETHING GOOD

LET IT BE PEACE

New edition 1966

Reproduced and Printed in Great Britain
by Latimer Trend & Co. Ltd., Whitstable

CHAPTER ONE

The Whare

ONCE UPON A TIME THERE WAS A little Maori boy named Wiremu, but he was called Wiri for short.

Wiri had a father and a mother, but he had so many brothers and sisters that it was hard work finding food for them all.

His uncle, Hori, had no children but he had room in his whare and plenty of food, so Wiri was given to his uncle. That is the Maori way.

The whare where Hori and Wiri lived was on a hill across the river from the pa. It was made of slabs which

Hori had collected from the old sawmill. The roof was made of iron which had fallen off the waggon on the rough road across the river, and the nails Hori had taken from Mr Waterford's woolshed as he passed one day; Mr Waterford was a kind man, he liked giving things to other people. By corry, Hori would give him a kit of kumara some day to make up for taking his nails.

In time, the rain and the wind and the sun had bleached the whare silver grey as a pigeon, and Hori and Wiri thought it was a very fine and beautiful home.

The inside was just as beautiful and fine as the outside. There were two rooms and Hori had lined the walls with smooth slabs, and made the floor of boards, which he had collected from the river after a flood.

One room was the bedroom, with two mattresses made of sacks stuffed with sheep's wool from Mr Waterford's shed. But Hori had bought the blankets himself with his shearing money, and they were brown with red and yellow and blue stripes. The pillows were made of sugar bags stuffed with wool and covered with white crochet pillow slips edged with red, which were made by Hori's cousin's aunt.

The other room had a big fire-place made from some

of the iron dropped by the waggon, and it was so wide that it held quite easily the logs of drift-wood they sledged up from the river. It also held the big black camp oven they used for cooking bread and meat and kumara. From the iron bar across the chimney hung three hooks like S's to hold the three black billies for tea-water and stews and puha.

The floor of the room was covered with a flax mat made by Tinopai, Wiri's grandmother. There was an old wooden chair for Hori and a box for Wiri to sit by the fire. There was a table and a form and a big tin basin for making the bread. There were a few knives and spoons about, and tin pannikins hanging on some of Mr Waterford's nails, and some plates on the table and some coats and shirts on other nails and tins on the mantel-piece. Also on the table was a candle held up between three nails. There was a big box where Hori kept every-thing in one corner, and in the other corner, there were a rifle and a slash-hook and a spade.

One of the walls had paper on it, patterned with people and horses and yachts, and flowering fruit trees with beautiful pakeha women.

King George the Fifth, Queen Mary, Pharlap, Lord

Liverpool, the *Mandalay* and the fruit trees and beautiful pakeha women, all came out of the *Weekly* which Mrs. Waterford sometimes handed on to Hori.

Everything, the billies and the pannikins, and the *Mandalay* seemed to float in a smoky haze, seemed blended by the mossy, flaxy, Maori smell and Wiri and Hori were quietly happy.

Tiger, the big brindled pig dog, and Miu, the black and white cat, were quietly happy too.

CHAPTER TWO

The River

THE RIVER WHICH RAN BELOW THE whare was a fine river. In winter it was a roaring swirl, yellow and angry as a Taniwha, but in summer it was dark green and quiet as moss. It was called the Waitukituki.

In winter and summer the river was always Hori's and Wiri's best and most generous friend, next of course, to the Waterfords.

It filled its flood waters with wood for their fire in winter and dragged boards from the flood gates and bridges. Then it licked higher and higher up its banks until the tongues of water tore the posts from Mr Waterford's fences and hurled them ashore again for Hori's scrub wall.

Sometimes it caught a sheep unawares and carried it down to the bend below the whare, so Hori and Wiri and Tiger and Miu had meat to eat and more wool to sleep on.

Once it rose high enough to wash away the Waterford's maize shed and Hori caught the cobs in his willow woven basket and put them away to plant in the spring.

"By corry, I give Mary Waterford some green maize in the summer—he like that."

In summer, Hori and Wiri would wade across the river, or jump from stone to stone if they wanted to keep dry. Or, they could ride across on Hini the old mare, leading her almost blind son Pikau with a pack saddle on his back.

But in winter, Hini and Pikau were kept in a paddock on the pa side of the river, so Wiri and Hori had to go across in the cage.

The cage had a board floor about two feet square and was hung to a pulley by wires from each corner. It slid across the river on a thick strong wire which was tied to a rimu tree on the whare side and to a totara tree on the pa side.

The wire was higher on the rimu than it was on the totara so that when Wiri and Hori and Tiger sat on the cage on the whare side it went whirring like a locust, so

fast across the river that Wiri felt as though his puku
had been left behind.

But when they came home, tired and wet and sleepy,
the cage wouldn't move when they sat on it. So Hori had
to pull and pull on a long rope tied to the rimu tree,
coiling it beside him until there was almost no room for
Wiri and Tiger. And Wiri was frightened of the roaring
blackness of the river at night, so he kept very close to
Hori as they went up the track from the cage.

He was tired and wobbly with sleep as he walked into
the whare. He tumbled on to his soft bed and burrowed
clothes and all into the stripy blankets and pulled them
close over his sleepy head . . . safe from the morepork
and the angry blackness of the river . . . and the taipo
and the taniwha. . . .

At his feet Tiger lay stretched out asleep, and Miu,
the black and white cat, was a soft sleeping ball behind
his pillow.

CHAPTER THREE

The River & Mrs Waterford

WHEN THE RIVER WAS GREEN AND quiet as moss, it ran softly between the boulders, gently brushing the waving tresses of the river slime. And Wiri played for hours in its warm waters, until the soles of his brown feet were pink as the underneaths of mushrooms.

He made boats of the thick flax sticks that grew beside the river. He cut the sticks, then sharpened the ends and hollowed out the pith until he had a whole fleet of canoes.

He piled some stones between two boulders so that the water deepened behind them, then fell with a tiny rush, down the other side. And he talked to himself in Maori pretending.

"I am the Great Chief, and these are my Warriors. He who can shoot over the Kata Kehua falls shall marry my beautiful daughter Tinopai, but the inside of the canoe must be untouched by water—the warrior must sit straight to sail the rapids below."

He put his canoes in the water and tried them over and over, till his bare brown back was burnt almost black with the sun, and the palms of his hands and feet were pink as the underneaths of mushrooms. But still none of his canoes could win the great chief's daughter. So he helped his favourite one by guiding it with a blade of grass and it won.

Then he pulled out some river slime and scrubbed and washed a boulder for the wedding feast. He went to the bank and collected watercress and river pipis from the mud, to put on the boulder table for the feast. But there came a thud, thud along the sand and splash, splash through the water and Tiger bounded on to the boulder and pushed the great feast into the water.

"Etama, Tiger! Etama!"

Tiger slithered about on the rock and licked Wiri's hot brown face, whining and barking as he looked up the river till Wiri looked too.

[9]

At the lower end of the pool above the crossing, Hori was bailing out his canoe, so Wiri ran along the bank and splashed through the water and climbed into the stern. Tiger struggled in too, shaking the water from his rough coat as he trotted to the bows.

Hori finished baling and paddled up the river, up the longest pool in the Waitukituki. The canoe was made by Toa, Hori's father, shaped and hollowed from a giant totara.

There were flax kits and hooks and lines in the canoe, and a hinake for trapping eels and some jam tins.

Wiri sat dragging his fingers through the deep cool

green water, listening to the soft splish-splash of the paddles. They passed below the Waterford's house. They passed below the woolshed and the dip and slid into the cool green darkness of the gorge. A mob of wild duck flew quacking from the water, and a water-rat scuttled along a mossy ledge into the maidenhair. "I hope I had a gun," whispered Wiri to himself.

Away ahead a trout rose, dimpling the water, caught at a beetle which dropped from a fern frond and darted to the bottom as the canoe came over. They slid round a corner and suddenly came aground in the blazing white sunlight of the open river bed.

Hori took two of the kits and Wiri followed him. They climbed up the bank through the koninis to the clump of wild cherry trees beyond. They ate and ate the fat red cherries till the juice made wet clean tracks from the corners of Wiri's mouth down his hot brown chin. And Hori ate just as many as Wiri, because they hadn't had any breakfast and they hadn't had any dinner and only eels and puha the night before.

When they were full, they filled their kits, carried them down to the canoe and floated easily down the river to the track leading up to the Waterford's.

Hori went first, carrying his kit of cherries, then Wiri, then Tiger.

They found Mrs Waterford picking sweet peas in her garden.

"Hello Hori! Hello Wiri, and Tiger too? What lovely cherries, Hori. Been to your secret place I suppose."

"For you Mary," said Hori.

"For me? Oh, Hori! Go round to the kitchen and have some dinner with the men, you must be tired."

So they ate their dinner. Kapai. Kapai. Lamb, mint sauce, green peas, new potatoes, apple pie, cream, and the shepherds talked all the time about dogs.

"Thank you. Kapai." Hori and Wiri left the men and the cook and went to find Mrs Waterford who was hosing the vegetables.

"Good cabbage, Mary."

"Yes, Hori, you must have some. Oh, and Hori, the boss said to give you a quarter of meat. And there's half a bag of flour you can have—the cook doesn't like the brand. You're looking thin Hori, you work too hard. Wiri, here's a white rose for your buttonhole—Oh! you haven't a buttonhole have you? Well! for your belt then, Wiri."

But Wiri held it in his hand, his belt was tight enough —and he followed Hori and his heavy load down to the river.

"By corry, Mary the good woman—I give him kumara in the autumn—all my kumara."

They loaded the canoe and floated silently down the river—the trout were jumping round them, silver sickles in the star-light. Wiri with his white flower sang softly to himself and Hori smoked peacefully, lazily steering the canoe with his paddle. In the bows, Tiger, the tense brindled figure-head, strained forward in the half-darkness. . . . On the whare door step, Miu the cat waited trustful and patient. . . .

CHAPTER FOUR

The Pakeha's Fish

IT WAS THE HOTTEST DAY OF SUMMER and the sun shone with orange fierceness through the smoke from the bush fires, and blazed on the roof of the whare, as though he was trying to melt Hori and Wiri who were eating their kai inside.

Wiri finished quickly and he called to Tiger, who lay sleeping between the maize stalks. He took a kit from under the whare and a flax eel line and they set off along the hot dusty track to the hill.

The summer grass, pale and bleached as toi-toi, was slippery as they climbed. They went over the hill into some manuka scrub and pushed their way into the bracken which grew high above their heads. They came to a steep bank, and Tiger struggled through the water-fern making a track for Wiri to the creek.

The cool stream rushed bubbling between the stones, swirling round Tiger, who had stretched himself in the water. Wiri sat on a boulder and scooped some water in his hands and threw it over his bracken powdered body, brown like the fronds of the water-fern.

When he was cooled, he tied his kit to his belt and wandered down the creek-bed, stooping to look for cray-fish under the stones. His hand, quick as a hawk, would pounce on their tails as they shot backwards from their rocky homes and soon his kit was filled with the green-brown crawling creatures.

"Kapai te koura! Haeremai Tiger," and they went down the creek to the river.

Wiri put down his kit and lay on the river bank. The hot air round him was filled with the scent of the penny royal, and the sleepy hum of the wild bees and the ziz-zizzing of the locusts. . . .

So still, so heavy, so hot. . . . At the mouth of the creek the fat trout lay feeding, sleepy and lazy, and across the river, the heat rose like a sheet of quivering glass.

"Ziz . . ziz . . . ziz . . . ziz . . z . . z . . S . . S." Wiri sat up and rubbed his eyes. That wasn't one of the sounds which go to make the great sleepy silence of midday. That wasn't the whirr of the army of locusts on the tree trunks. That was a pakeha fishing up the river, flicking his line over the water as Rangi, the bullock driver, flicked his long whip down the smooth backs of the bullocks. But the trout still slept in the cool deep water, undisturbed—too lazy to rise.

Wiri took out his flax eel line. He would fish too and catch a big, big eel for Hori—Hori, he like tuna.

So he picked a pipi from the sand and cracked it on a stone. He fixed the juicy bait to his eel hook and let the line down, down into the deep green water.

Up the river, the pakeha's line softly whistled across the water and Wiri's pipi dropped into the green as he tried another place. By corry, what a tug, what a big, big eel he must have caught this time. He gripped his line and peered into the green water to see the struggling monster. But it wasn't a big eel at all, it was a giant brown trout caught unawares in the sleepy heat of the day.

Wiri held tight to the line and walked along the river bank, dragging the heavy plunging weight down stream. He came to where the water shallowed and dragged the flapping fish on to the sand while Tiger barked till the rocks echoed with the noise. And from the bank the pakeha shouted.

"Hi! can't you keep that dog quiet? By jove! what's that? A twelve pounder! What's your fly boy?"

Wiri stared.

"What fly did you hook him with?" Wiri held up his flax line.

"But, I say, you can't do that old chap, it's not sporting, you know—it's against the law!"

Wiri still stared. He was mad, the pakeha man, porangi.

"I say, you must put it back, but we'll weigh him first. He'll go twelve if an ounce!" And he pulled out his tiny weighing machine and lifted the trout with the hook.

"By gad! a pretty fish, eleven and threequarters, my word, you're a clever boy!" And he searched in his pockets. "Will you take this for your fish?" He held up a pound note.

Wiri looked at the man and he looked at the fish and he looked at the pound note. That's what Hori would like. So he took the note and ran along the river bank and up the hill to the maize patch where Hori was

[17]

working. He pushed the pound into Hori's hand and gabbled in Maori until he had told him all about it. Hori chuckled and was pleased as he patted his head. "By corry, you the good boy!" and he was proud of Wiri.

But this isn't the end of the story, because Hori was at the Waterford's six months later and when he was leaving Mrs Waterford said:

"Hori, here's a meat pie for you and there's part of a bag of flour and some warm shirts I cut down for Wiri. Oh! and Hori, a bundle of magazines I thought you might like to see."

So Hori took the pie and the flour and the shirts and the magazines and trudged down the road through the mud and rain and down the track to the river. He put his load on the cage and pulled himself over and tied the cage to the rimu tree. He climbed up the slippery track to the whare and went inside. He lit the candle and made some tea in the billy, and he and Wiri sat by the fire and ate slice after slice of Mrs Waterford's pie, because they hadn't had any breakfast or any dinner and only kumara and puha the night before.

When they were finished, Hori lit his pipe and they

looked at the papers Mrs Waterford had given them. Some were from England and Wiri liked the beautiful pakeha women in their fine clothes with beads round their necks.

He liked the pakeha men too, riding on horses as smooth and shiny as flax. And the men with their fishing rods like the pakeha up the river.

He saw a picture of a man like the pakeha, standing by a tree fern and holding up a big, brown trout—and he looked harder because it was his pakeha and it was his fish.

So he showed it to Hori, and Hori read the writing underneath the picture which said:

"Mr Maurice Laird, the well-known angler, with a fourteen pound brown trout which he took from the Waitukituki river, on a recent visit to New Zealand."

Then Hori laughed and laughed till you couldn't hear the rain on the roof or the angry roar of the river, but only Hori laughing.

He took his knife and cut out the picture. He mixed some flour and water and smeared it on the back and pasted it on the wall beside the King and the *Mandalay* and the fruit trees and beautiful pakeha women.

He stroked the little boy's hair as he gazed proudly at the picture, and better than anyone else in the world Wiri loved Hori.

Tiger, the pig dog, pushed his head under Hori's other hand, and by the fire that sleepy ball Miu opened an eye for a moment and shut it again, because more than anything else in the world, Miu loved sleeping.

CHAPTER FIVE

Tinopai

THE COOL SPRING AIR WHISPERED softly among the pale plumes of the toi-toi and played gently with Hini's dark mane as she stood carved like rock against the first pale-clear light of morning.

Hori climbed the hill and put on her bridle, and led her to the whare. He pulled out the saddle and put it on her back and did up the girth.

He took a sack with both ends sewn up and a split in the middle of one side, and he tied it on to his saddle. This was his pikau for carrying home the flour and sugar he was going to the town to buy. For the flour and sugar he meant to buy to fill his empty flour box and his empty sugar tin.

He called to Wiri and lifted him behind the saddle. He called to Tiger and tied him under the whare. He led Hini to the step and climbed on between Wiri and the pikau and they rode off down the track and across the river.

As they went up the long hill above the Waterford's, they looked back at the beauty of the morning. The rising sun had drawn the mist from the river bed and left it floating like fleeces above the sleeping pa.

Hini neighed loudly to a piebald mare who was feeding with her foal on the hill, and a family of hares caught at their play, crouched with silly flattened ears as they passed. But, by corry, what was that! a sparrow hawk swooped, pecked at Hori's hat and flew screeching to his nest in a tall dead tree.

They rode slowly down into the sun-flecked green of the bush. A fantail fluttered ahead, chattering as she led them away through the shadow and the sunlight and the tumult of bird-songs, to the lake, lying like a slab of greenstone in its setting of raupo. Like greenstone fringed with the pink lake weed. With wild duck floating still and flat as though carved on its smooth green surface. With pukekos on its swampy edge, stalking blue and white on their scarlet legs, always searching in the pinkness.

[22]

Then Wiri sang, by corry he sang, to frighten away the big taniwha his grandmother had told him about. The big dragon she said was hiding beneath the still lake water.

When they left the lake the road ran out of the bush into the open country, and Wiri grew very tired as they rode up the long hill. As they neared the top the bushes beside them had a grey dry look and the banks of the road were very white. The warm air was heavy with sulphur and a big yellow board on the roadside said:

```
3 Miles
To the famous
TE PUNA
HOT SPRINGS
New Zealand's Wonder
Spot
Superior Accommodation
at
reasonable prices
GET WELL AT TE PUNA
                    A.A.
```

Just past the notice, they turned off and went along a track through the manuka bushes, because Wiri was to be left with his grandmother, Tinopai, and in a moment they would see her whare.

In a moment, they did see her whare, and there was Tinopai, wise, kind, comfortable Tinopai, standing in her doorway watching them. Her face was shining like polished copper. Her eyes were still and deep as the river, and her thoughts shone in her eyes like patches of light in a river pool. Her hair hung in greying plaits over the shoulders of her loose red blouse and her feet were bare beneath the full blue skirt.

She walked slowly to meet them and shook Hori's hand and pressed her nose to his. She stooped and murmured to Wiri as she took him by the hand and led him into the whare. She made them some tea and fed them on raisin bread and all the time she and Hori talked to each other in Maori.

When he had finished Hori got on his horse and rode off towards the town. Then Tinopai lifted Wiri to her knee and stroked his hair and rocked him as she sang her strange old Maori songs, till Wiri thought in all the world there was no one as comfortable as Tinopai.

When he was rested she put him down and took a flax kit from a nail. She wrapped some meat in a piece of sack and put it in the kit, then she filled it with kumara and potato. She led Wiri along the white track until she came to a bubbling pool in a small clearing. Out of the pool came clouds of steam, spurting forth like the angry breath of the taniwha, and Wiri shrank back in fear.

"By corry, I keep away."

But Tinopai laughed and walked firmly to the edge of the pool. She pulled some flax and tied one end to her kit and the other end she tied to a manuka bush; then she lowered her kit into the pool. She turned back to Wiri and took him down the steaming stream to where it widened and he took off his clothes and ran splashing into the hot water. Then Tinopai picked up some red stones and threw them into a deeper pool and Wiri dived and came up laughing and bubbling with the stones in his hand.

"You the good boy," and she left him in the water and walked up to the whare and came back with two kits full of clothes and a long bar of yellow soap.

She squatted on a flat rock on the edge of the pool and one by one she washed the clothes, dipping them in the hot water then soaping them on a rock. When she had finished she spread them on the bushes to dry.

She called to Wiri and she rubbed him all over with
her soap and washed him. Then she floated him on his
back in the water and she soaped and rinsed his hair till
the pool was filled with bubbles. She took him out and
dried him with a big stripy towel, and Wiri let her do
this, because in all the world there was no one as calm
and comfortable as Tinopai.

They walked up the stream to where the boiling spring
bubbled out of the depths of the earth to cook the dinner
for Tinopai. She lifted out her kit and left it for a
moment to cool then carried it along to the whare. She
filled two plates with the steaming kai and Wiri ate till
he could eat no more. When they had finished they took

their plates and pannikins to the creek and washed them in the warm water and carried them back to the whare.

Tinopai lit her old black pipe and pulled a half-made kit to her as she sat on the mat in the whare. Wiri sat on the doorstep watching her quick fingers plaiting in and out, the strands she worked with quickly shaping into the side of a kit and the strands that waited firmly held down with her wide strong toes. Between the puffs she talked to him in her grand and beautiful Maori, and told him the story he loved.

"Oh, my child, Wiremu, listen to the story I am about to tell you. Your great grandfather Mauri was brave and strong. He was the chief of our great tribe. He was good and kind. He had four sons and one daughter. She was very beautiful. Her name was Tinopai because she was as good as she was beautiful. The young chiefs who were followers of Mauri all fell in love with Tinopai. There was much fighting between them. So Mauri called his followers together and said to them: 'Oh, my kinsmen, listen to the words I am about to speak to you. Behold Tinopai, my beloved daughter, who stands by my side. To him who can shoot over the Kata Kehua falls I give her in marriage, but the inside of the canoe must be untouched by water and the warrior must sit straight to the rapids below.'

"He had ceased speaking. For a moment it seemed that no one dared shoot the falls to win Tinopai. Then a warrior came forward. He was young and handsome, brave and strong. The whole tribe knew him to be kind, good and gracious. His name was Toa. He was the only one brave enough to shoot the falls and he won the good and beautiful Tinopai. Wherefore, oh my child, Wiremu, you must be like Toa, strong and gracious and brave and good."

As Wiri sat filled with her story he saw her push aside her flax kit and sit puffing her pipe, her eyes still and deep as the river, and her thoughts shining in her eyes like patches of light on a river pool. . . .

Then Hori rode up the track.

He tied Hini to a bush and took a bulging sugar bag from one side of the pikau and a cardboard box from the other and he went into the whare.

He untied the string from the bulging bag and pulled out two big red crayfish for Tinopai. He opened the cardboard box and took out some of the pink iced cakes and put them on a plate. He opened his parcel and gave

Tinopai a length of yellow silk and he wound a bright red scarf round Wiri's neck and all the time he talked a lot and was very kind.

When they had eaten, and drunk their tea, Hori put his bulging bag and his box of cakes into the pikau, and Tinopai waved to them as they rode off.

Wiri clung tightly to Hori's tweed coat as they jogged along, and he felt very happy and very clean and very tired.

Hori sang and talked for a while, then he grew tired, too, and quiet, because he began to think about the empty sugar tin and the empty flour box and his empty pockets.

Mrs Waterford was at the gate as they passed, waiting for the mail.

"Hori, will you come and do some digging for me next week? And you could put in the kumaras too, Hori, they never grow for me. Oh, and bring Wiri along too, because Miss Helen's boy is staying with me. He's a spoilt town boy Wiri, he thinks there's nothing to do here— he'll learn a lot from you. Look, he's sleepy Hori."

So Hori moved him gently to the front of his saddle.

"I come on Monday," he said. "I like to see Helen's

[29]

boy," and when he rode off, his pockets didn't feel quite so empty.

They crossed the river and climbed slowly up the hill to the whare, and Hori carried the little sleepy Wiri and put him on his bed. He pulled the blankets over him and the brown eyelids wavered a second then sank to rest over the soft dark eyes. . . .

Hori pulled the smouldering logs together and blew them into a blaze. He put on the billy for his tea, while Tiger, poor left behind Tiger, sat happily watching. And Miu the sleepy-one, wound round the old man's legs rubbing and purring her love . . . purring and rubbing her great love . . . because Miu was hungry.

CHAPTER SIX

Wiri & Anthony

IT WAS A BRIGHT BLUE DAY, SPARKLING and clear after the Sunday's rain and Mary Waterford was early in her garden.

"Anthony," she called through the window. "Come outside, it's lovely."

"No," said Anthony, "it's cold." She went inside. "Anthony, come along."

"I want to go home," he said, "this place is silly, there's nothing to do. I wish I could've brought my train —why wouldn't they let me?" But he followed her out.

"Hello, here's Wiri, Anthony. He's Hori's little boy— Hori's going to dig the garden for me so they'll be living in our shearer's whare for a week."

"Hello Wiri, I've got a train at home and a meccano, and I go to the pictures on Saturdays, and I'm going to have a bike next year."

"Show him the whare, Wiri."

They went over the paddock.

"Is this the whare? What a dirty place, you couldn't live here. We've got a refrigerator at home and we have ice cream. My daddy's got a . . . what's in that box?" And he pointed to a square box which Hori had used to bring his treasures from his own whare.

Wiri opened the lid and Tony saw some tobacco tins and knives and magazines and in the middle was a big glittering lump of yellow gum. "Oh, boy! what's that? Gold? Why its bigger than the lump Black Pete found in my comic. Where did your father find it? Is it really pure gold?"

"Kauri gum," said Wiri.

"Gum? Well, *I* believe it's real gold. Do you think I could come and stay here with you?—it's not much good over at the house. I'll get my mother to send up my train and we could run it round this floor. Where are you going?"

"To the river."

"Oh! couldn't we stay here? I'll show you where the lines could go—it's all muddy down at the river, isn't it?" But Wiri was already on the track leading to his river,

[32]

and Anthony followed, slowly picking his way through the puddles.

"Take off the shoe." Wiri looked at Tony's feet.

"Ooo, but it's muddy. . . . All right, I'll take them off; you don't wear shoes, do you Wiri . . . oooo it's squelchy, isn't it? What's that sort of bell noise?"

"Bell-bird, he sing," said Wiri.

"Bell-bird. Oh! I've seen a picture of one. I didn't know they were here. What's that?" A lawyer vine had climbed up a tree looking for light, and still growing had reached to a tree across the track, and its strong old vine dropped in a loop between the two.

Wiri sat on the swing it made and swung himself high into the air.

"We've got a good swing at school—its got real rope and . . . Wiri, can I come on too?" So Wiri let Anthony sit on the swing and he stood up behind him and worked his legs and arms till they flew through the air.

"Higher, Wiri, higher, we'll soon swing across the river. This is a good swing isn't it, Wiri?"

They left the swing and went down the track to the river to where Hori's canoe was tied to the roots of a totara tree.

[33]

"Whose boat is that?"

"Hori's canoe."

"Can we go in it?"

"To-morrow. I take you hunt pig."

"I won't be allowed—oh, yes, Mary'll let me. We'll hunt pigs to-morrow, won't we Wiri. What are you doing?"

"Making boat," and Tony watched him make his fleet of flax stick canoes.

"Yes, let's play wharves. If I had my blue train we could run it along the wharves. What are you doing with those stones?"

"Making the waterfall."

So they played for hours, sailing the small canoes over the Kata Kehua falls, and as usual the brave warrior Toa had to be helped over with a straw of grass. Then they washed and scrubbed a boulder for the wedding feast. But a bell clanged in the distance and Anthony said: "That's not a bell-bird is it Wiri?"

"No, dinner."

So they ran up the track and across the paddock to the garden and Tony said: "Mary, can I have lunch in the kitchen with Wiri, I can't wait for you and Uncle Miles?"

"Yes, of course you can."

So off they went to eat their lunch. Kapai. Kapai—

oh boy, oh boy, what a lunch. And one of the shepherds who was called Pat, said: "It's good for the kid, he's a decent little chap, but he's been brought up like a blinking girl. We'll have to put you on a bucking horse, Tony."

"All right," said Tony. "When?"

"Wiri," laughed Pat, "you can come mustering after lunch if you like. You ride the roan pony and I'll carry the kid."

So they saddled the horses and rode off over the hills, Wiri on the pony and Anthony clinging tightly to the front of Pat's saddle. Behind them the pack of dogs trotted hanging their tongues.

Halfway up a hill they stopped and Pat sent two of the dogs to muster the sheep from the hill tops until the ridges were white with the moving mobs of sheep and lambs being driven to the docking yards below. Anthony gripped the saddle, silent with excitement, and forgot all about the blue train in his nursery at home.

When the sheep were yarded Wiri took him up the creek and they played in the water—lifting up the stones to see the small crayfish shoot backwards from their homes. They poked about under the banks to make the long thin greeny-black eels slide from their hiding places and Anthony shrieked with laughter till the banks echoed with the sound.

When the sun left the creek, they went back to the yards. The sheep had been turned out and Henry, the cowboy, was saddling his horse to go home. He lifted Tony on in front. Wiri caught the pony and they rode down towards the cow paddock. The cows were at the gate so they drove them through and into the cow yard. Henry got the buckets and began to milk, *tin*-tin-*tin*-tin. Wiri ran over to the whare for two pannikins and Henry filled them with foaming milk.

"Henry," said Anthony, "why do cows have horns?"

"To blow when they're far away in the bush," said Henry.

"Why do they want to blow them?"

"To call themselves home to dinner and there's Mrs Waterford calling you to dinner, so hop it, my lad, or I won't take you sledging firewood to-morrow."

"Couldn't I just run over and see Hori's gold before I go to bed?" But Mary said:

"No, not till to-morrow." So he climbed into bed and in two minutes he was fast asleep.

The Pig Hunters

THE MORNING WAS BRILLIANT WITH spring as Mary Waterford went over to the kumara patch.

"Good morning, Hori, I suppose those boys went off with Henry, did they? They say they're going pig-hunting in the river bush after lunch. Oh dear, there are never any pigs as far down as that, are there, Hori? I don't want to stop them, because it's so good for Tony to rough it. He's been very spoilt, Hori—not like Wiri. He did nothing but whine the first day because he hadn't brought his beloved blue train with him."

"Tony the fine boy," said Hori. "I go to the Store on Friday. I like Helen's boy. He go home Saturday?"

"Yes. . . . Hori, I never know what you do to kumaras to make them grow—you must have magic fingers. Hello Wiri—hello Tony—what do you want?"

"Mary can we have our lunch? We're going hunting pigs and Wiri says if you give us chops we can light a fire and cook them. What about Tiger, Wiri, will he need a chop too—he has to do all the work Mary—he's the one that catches the pigs, not us."

So Mary packed them each a parcel of lunch and gave Wiri a box of matches. "Tony, for goodness sake, do everything Wiri tells you," she said, as she followed them down to the river. She watched Wiri help Tony into the canoe. Tiger jumped in too and Wiri paddled them across the river, over the longest pool in the Waitukituki. He tied the canoe to a bush on the other side. Then Tiger ran along ahead, sniffing, sniffing for pig.

When they had been climbing for a quarter of an hour, Tony said:

"It's great fun hunting pig, isn't it, Wiri? But I think we'd better have our lunch now, don't you?"

They gathered some dry sticks and built a fire. Wiri made Tony keep away while he lit it, and Tony danced with excitement when he saw the blaze. They put on more wood and ate their sandwiches, till the fire was hot enough to cook their chops.

Then they found two sticks and poked them into the

fatty end of each chop and dangled them in the fire. And oh the sizzling wonderful smell as they cooked; and oh the luscious juicy burntness when they ate them. Kapai, kapai. Oh boy, oh boy, and in all his life Tony had never tasted anything so perfect.

"I'm pretty full, Wiri, are you? It makes you a bit sleepy doesn't it?" So they lay on a soft bed of leaves and were soon sound asleep. And the weka who stalked out to eat the crumbs thought they were "bush babies," one brown, one white, because no one had told him they were two mighty pig-hunters.

"By corry, Tony, wake up! Hi, Tony, pig!" Wiri pulled Tony up and the bush was filled with Tiger's furious barking.

"The tree Tony, by corry we climb the tree." They ran to a hou-hou and Wiri pulled Tony up after him, while all the time the air was filled with Tiger's barks and could you believe it, the angry snorting grunts of a PIG ! !

"I hope I had a gun," said Wiri. "Would I shoot that pig and take him home to Hori." Tony was shaking with excitement.

"I wish I had a gun too—I'd soon shoot him! We would, wouldn't we Wiri?"

The noise grew louder and louder as Tiger chased the pig crashing through the undergrowth, nearer and nearer to the boys.

"It sounds as big as an elephant, Wiri. Are wild pigs very big?"

"Yes," said Wiri. "They big, big pig."

"Are they black, Wiri, awfully black?"

"Sometime they are."

"Pigs have tusks don't they, Wiri, big ones, like a sort of rhinoceros, aren't they?"

"Yes, boar, he have the big, big tusk."

"Do pigs ever kill people, Wiri, with their tusks?"

"One Maori, he get kill—he no gun."

"Can pigs climb trees, Wiri. . . . O-ooo Wiri, its coming close—it's here, Wiri!" . . . And rushing below them came a huge black boar with Tiger barking at its heels. Down, down they crashed through the bush and out of sight. Gradually, the crashing stopped and there was only the sound of Tiger's angry barks and the desperate snorting grunts of the trapped pig.

"Tiger, he baled him up by the rock," said Wiri. "We have to stay here all night till someone come."

"My mother will be asleep in bed then, won't she, Wiri. . . . Wiri, will someone come? . . . Wiri . . . " and Tony's voice trembled and wouldn't work any more.

"You the big boy, Tony. Hori come soon, he hear Tiger bark. You take your mother a big, big pair tusk when you go home—and when you go home, you have ice cream and you play with your blue train—I hope I had a blue train—he have the real engine?"

"Yes. Will Hori come soon?"

"BANG ! ! " The noise of the shot thundered round the rocks below them and faded thinly through the trees. Then Hori's voice echoed.

"Haeremai, Wiremu!"

"Hi, Hori!" And the two boys scrambled down the tree and ran to meet him. Then they all went together to where the pig lay—and Hori patted their heads and talked laughingly to them and in all the world there were never two prouder pig hunters than Anthony and Wiremu.

CHAPTER EIGHT

Hori's Gold

IT WAS FRIDAY AFTERNOON AND THE garden lay sleeping softly in the warm spring sunshine. From the river the happy shouts of the boys floated through the air and the trees stood hard and clear against the blue satin of the sky. Somewhere, the pipi-pipi, that ever greedy stranger, shrilled tui-tui-ti-u for his food and Hori unbent from the last long line of kumara.

Mary's kumara would grow this time. By corry, they would. They had been planted by Hori's magic fingers and the pipi-pipi had sung his song.

The old man put away his spade and went into the whare. He came out with something bulky wrapped in a sugar bag and he set off along the three miles to the store.

When the pale blue sky had turned to primrose behind

the dark patterns of the trees, Hori came home.

He went over to the house and handed Mrs Waterford a parcel. "For Tony," he said. "He the fine boy."

"Oh, Hori, what have you brought?—I'll just give it to Tony, he's having his tea." And Hori went off to his whare.

Tony opened his parcel.

"Mary, Mary, Hori's brought me a blue train—much better than my one at home. But I'm going to give it to Wiri—he does want a train."

So when he had finished he ran over to the whare with his new blue train.

"Hori, thank you for the train, it's much better than my one at home—its got more carriages—it's a beauty. But I'm going to give it to Wiri, Hori, because I've got my tusks to take home and lots of flax canoes."

He showed Wiri how to wind the train and it ran merrily round and round the whare floor. Tiger got up with a groan and went outside, and Miu the black and white one, jumped on a box and waved her tail backwards and forwards, swish, swish . . . because Miu was angry.

When it was too dark to see any longer, Wiri took his

train and sat on the step by Hori and on the other side Tony pressed up close beside the old man's tweed coat.

"Hori, could I hold your gold just once more before I go home?" Hori puffed at his pipe in silence and Tony went and felt in the treasure box.

"Hori, it's gone, your lovely gold's gone, Hori. Wherever is it?"

"He go away," said Hori. "You come home now, Tony, Mary, he want you go to bed. You come again in the summer, and we go hunt more pig."

When Tony climbed into bed he said: "Mary, d'you know, I think Hori bought my train with his lump of gold. You'll get it back for him, won't you, Mary, it's his very greatest treasure, he got it for saving a gumdigger's life."

"Dear old Hori, Tony. Yes, I'll get it back, I promise I won't forget." And Tony snuggled down happily between the sheets.

Over at the whare Hori sat dreaming by the fire. . . . under the stripy blankets Wiri was fast asleep with Tiger at his feet. At his head, that angry cat Miu sat swishing her tail, because under her pillow, her very own pillow, lay hard and lumpy—the little blue train.

CHAPTER NINE

Hari-Mutunga-Kore

So, ONCE UPON A TIME, THERE WAS
Wiremu, who lived with his uncle in their silver
grey whare.

The river which ran below the whare was the Waitukituki. In winter it swirled between its banks, yellow and
angry as a taniwha—and in summer it flowed gently—
green and quiet as moss.

They found eels in the river and sometimes, as you
know, a big brown trout. They sailed on its long smooth
waters and they used it for their bath. In summer and
in winter, it filled its waters with food for them and with
boards for their whare and posts for their fences.

Always it was kind. Like Mary Waterford, it was
always kind and generous and Hori and Wiri were

[46]

quietly happy. They took what they were given and they either gave what they had or they meant to give what they had, which is the Maori way.

When they had money, they spent it. They went to town to buy, or meaning to buy, flour for their box and sugar for their tin. On the way they saw Tinopai, wise, kind Tinopai, with her eyes as deep as the river, and her thoughts shining in her eyes like patches of light.

Then came Tony and the little blue train and Tiger groaned sometimes, while Miu, the sleepy one, swished her tail because she didn't-like-little-blue-trains-under-her-pillow.

The shining cuckoo, the ever greedy pipi-pipi, had sung his song and Mary Waterford's kumara were planted by Hori's magic fingers, so they left the shearer's whare and went down the track to the canoe.

As they floated down the stream, the sun sank brilliant as fire behind the soft layers of the blue and purple hills and the river was dark and green as treacle. Treacle green, with patches of red light thrown on its waters. Stretched red on its waters like flat harmless patterns of the taniwha.

And Hori lazily steered with his paddle as he smoked

—stroking the sleek back of Miu as he dreamed, while in the bows, Tiger, like a carved Maori figure-head, stared into the distance.

No sound, but the hush-hushing of the river and the faint tui-tui-ti . . u of the pipi-pipi singing in her sleep and the small soft voice of Wiri in the stern.

"The pipi-pipi sing, Hori, the summer he come," and he was big inside with content, because more than anything else in the world he loved . . . everything.

The fiery colour faded from behind the darkening hills and the primrose sky was soft and clear with promise.

SOME MAORI WORDS

Here is a list of the Maori words used in *The Book of Wiremu*.

The meaning of the words is as correct as possible, but the pronunciation is just the pakeha-Maori which most of us use.

The syllables in Maori are not accented, but in "pakeha-Maori" we put a very slight accent on some syllables. These syllables have been printed in different type to show, for example, that the sweet potato "kumara" is pronounced "*koo*mara" rather than "koo*mara*."

The Maori words should be spoken quickly.

S.M.

THE LIST

By corry	(By golly)	very frequent expression
Etama	(*E*tarma)	"get away with you !"
Haeremai	(*Hi*-re-my)	Come here
Hari-mutunga-kore		joy-ending-not
Hinake	(*He*-na-kay)	eel trap
Hini	(*Hin*ny)	the mare's name
Hou hou	(Ho-ho)	tree
Hori	(*Horry*)	George
Kai	(Kie)	food
Kapai	(Ka-pie)	good
Kata Kehua	(*Kutta-Kay*hooa)	Laughing Ghost waterfall
Kauri	(*Kow*ry)	tree
Konini	(*Ko*ninny)	native fuchsia
Koura	(*Koo*ra)	crayfish

Kumara	(*Koo*mara)	sweet potato
Manuka	(*Ma*nooka)	scrub
Miu	(*Mee*-oo)	the cat's name
Pa	(Pa)	Maori village
Pikau	(Peekow)	the pack-horse's name
Pipi	(*Pi*ppy)	shellfish
Pipi-pipi	(*Pi*ppy-*pi*ppy)	pipipipiwhararoa, shining cuckoo
Puha	(*Poo*-ha)	sow-thistle; Maori cabbage
Pukeko	(*Poo*keko)	swamp hen
Puku	(*Poo*koo)	tummy
Rangi	(*Rang*-y)	sky
Raupo	(*Rau*po)	reeds
Rimu	(*Ree*moo)	tree
Taipo	(*Ty*-po)	imaginary monster
Taniwha	(*Ta*ne*fa*)	imaginary monster
Tinopai	(*Te*-no-pie)	Wiri's grandmother
Toa	(*To*a)	brave
Toe-toe	(Toy-toy)	native pampas grass
Totara	(*To*tara)	tree
Tuna	(*Too*na)	eel
Waitukituki	(*Wy*-*too*ky-tooky)	the river's name
Whare	(*Wa*rry)	Maori house
Wiremu	(*Wi*rrymoo)	William